T. REX
TRICK-OR-TREATS

by Lois G. Grambling · illustrated by Jack E. Davis

KATHERINE TEGEN BOOKS
An Imprint of HarperCollins*Publishers*

To Lara, Ty, Mason and Jesse . . . four VERY SPECIAL people.
Who are they? My grandchildren, of course!
—L.G.G.

For Kelly, Donna and Posie
—J.D.

T. Rex Trick-or-Treats
Text copyright © 2005 by Lois G. Grambling
Illustrations copyright © 2005 by Jack E. Davis
Printed in the United States

For information address HarperCollins Children's Books, a division of HarperCollins
Publishers, 1350 Avenue of the Americas, New York, NY 10019.
www.harperchildrens.com

Library of Congress Cataloging-in-Publication Data
Grambling, Lois G.
   T. rex trick-or-treats / Lois Grambling ; illustrated by Jack E. Davis.— 1st ed.
     p.   cm.
   Summary: A Tyrannosaurus rex cannot decide what kind of costume to wear on
Halloween night.
   ISBN 0-06-050252-5 — ISBN 0-06-050253-3 (lib. bdg.)
   [1. Dinosaurs—Fiction. 2. Tyrannosaurus rex—Fiction. 3. Halloween—Fiction.]
I. Davis, Jack E., ill. II. Title.
PZ7.G7655Tab 2005   2004022682
[E]—dc22   CIP
                                                  AC

Typography by Jeanne L. Hogle
1 2 3 4 5 6 7 8 9 10

First Edition

T. REX
TRICK-OR-TREATS

It was the darkest night of the year.
It was the scariest night of the year.
It was . . .

HALLOWEEN!

T. Rex finished carving his jack-o'-lantern.
It had
LONG
SHARP
POINTY
TEETH!
Just like his.

He stuck a candle in it and put it in the window.

"EEEEK!" screamed some trick-or-treaters passing by.

T. Rex was going trick-or-treating later that night with his friends.

But he hadn't decided what to wear.

He knew, though, that he wanted to wear something that would make him look

"Maybe I can wear a white sheet and be a
ghost," T. Rex said.
"That would make me look SCARY!"
But then he remembered.
His friend Diplodocus was going to wear a
white sheet and be a ghost.

"Maybe I can wear something with bones painted on it and be a skeleton," T. Rex said.

"That would make me look SCARY!"

But then he remembered.

His friend Stegosaurus was going to wear something with bones painted on it and be a skeleton.

"Maybe I can wear a pointy hat and be a witch," T. Rex said.

"That would make me look SCARY!"

But then he remembered.

His friend Iguanodon was going to wear a pointy hat and be a witch.

T. Rex was beginning to worry.
What *would* he wear tonight?
Just then his doorbell rang.

"TRICK OR TREAT!" shouted a scary ghost that was his friend Diplodocus.

"TRICK OR TREAT!" shouted a scary skeleton that was his friend Stegosaurus.

"TRICK OR TREAT!" shouted a scary witch that was his friend Iguanodon.

T. Rex invited them in.

"You aren't dressed!" said Diplodocus.

"I haven't decided what to wear," said T. Rex.

"Decide soon or all the treats will be gone!" said Iguanodon.

T. Rex didn't want that to happen.

"Do you have any suggestions?" he asked.

"Maybe you could wear a pair of giant wings and be a bat," said Diplodocus.

"Not SCARY enough!" said T. Rex, FROWNING.

"Maybe you could wear some twitchy whiskers and be a black cat," said Stegosaurus.

"Not SCARY enough!" said T. Rex, frowning a BIG FROWN.

"Maybe you could wear a carved-out pumpkin and carry a candle and be a jack-o'-lantern, like the one in your window," said Iguanodon.

"EEEEK!" screamed some passing trick-or-treaters. "Not SCARY enough!" said T. Rex, frowning a VERY BIG FROWN.

Diplodocus and Stegosaurus and Iguanodon stared at their friend.

"Maybe you should go trick-or-treating tonight as yourself, wearing just that VERY BIG FROWN," they said.

"I don't want to go trick-or-treating tonight as myself, wearing just this VERY BIG FROWN!" T. Rex said.

"I want to go trick-or-treating wearing something that will make me look SCARY!"

Diplodocus and Stegosaurus and Iguanodon stared at their friend again.

"Wearing that VERY BIG FROWN you *do* look SCARY," they said.

T. Rex looked in the mirror.

"EEEEK!"

he screamed.

"I do."

"And with you wearing that **VERY BIG FROWN** . . ."
said Diplodocus.

"Looking so VERY SCARY . . ." said Stegosaurus.

"What do you think we'll get when we ring doorbells tonight?" said Iguanodon.

"LOTS OF TREATS!" said T. Rex.

Later that dark Halloween night, as soon as their trick-or-treat bags filled up (and they filled up FAST), T. Rex stopped FROWNING and started smiling.

"EEEEK!" screamed some late trick-or-treaters staring up at Tyrannosaurus Rex's

LONG
    SHARP
        POINTY
            TEETH!

"EEEEK!" they screamed again, as they hurried off into the darkness.

Diplodocus and Stegosaurus and Iguanodon stared at their friend.

"Maybe next Halloween . . ." said Diplodocus.

"Instead of wearing a VERY BIG FROWN . . ." said Stegosaurus.

"You should wear that VERY BIG SMILE!" said Iguanodon.

"Now that would really be SCARY!" the three friends said. T. Rex said he would think about it.